]  R

LUTON
BOROUGH COUNCIL

ORCHARD

D1347510

ORCHARD BOOKS
338 Euston Road, London NW1 3BH
*Orchard Books Australia*
Hachette Children's Books
Level 17/207 Kent Street, Sydney NSW 2000

First published by Orchard Books in 1994
This edition published in 2008

Text © Rose Impey 1994
Illustrations © Shoo Rayner 2002

The rights of Rose Impey to be identified as the author and
Shoo Rayner to be identified as the illustrator of this Work
have been asserted by them in accordance with the
Copyright, Designs and Patents Act, 1988.

A CIP catalogue record for this book is available from the British Library.

ISBN 978 1 40830 296 5

1 3 5 7 9 10 8 6 4 2
Printed in China

Orchard Books is a division of Hachette Children's Books,
an Hachette Livre UK company.
www.hachettelivre.co.uk

# Sleepy Sammy

Sloths move very sl-o-w-ly.
In fact they hardly move at all.
Sloths are just about
the sleepiest animals in the world.
And Sammy Sloth was
the sleepiest sloth of all.

Hour after hour,
day after day,
week after week,
the Sloth family
hung upside down
at the top of a very tall tree.

There was Mr Sloth and Mrs Sloth

and Sammy Sloth

and Sammy's brothers and sisters.

Sloths don't *do* very much.
Mostly they eat and sleep,
and sleep and eat,
and…*(yawn)*…eat
and…*(yawn)*…sleep.

Yawn.

And sloths don't *go* anywhere much,
unless they have to.
Of course, sometimes,
they have to go
to the toilet.

Once a week the Sloth family
climbed slowly down
from the top
of the very tall tree
all the way to the ground.
Just to go to the toilet.

And then sl-o-w-ly,
v-e-r-y sl-o-w-ly,
they climbed
all the way back.

Then they hung there.

Yes, that's right,
eating and sleeping,
sleeping and eating,
and so on and so on.

No one said to Sammy,
"Sammy, wash your face.

Sammy, clean your teeth.

Sammy, tidy your room.

Sammy, take the dog for a walk."

In fact no one said anything much
to Sammy.

So Sammy just hung there
sleeping and dreaming.
Sammy had wonderful dreams.

He dreamed about being
the best footballer in the world,

or the most daring stuntman,

or the first sloth in space,

or the richest pop singer.

Sammy's dreams were so good
he didn't want to wake up.
He almost stopped eating.
He wouldn't make the trip
to the toilet.

Come on
Sammy.

All day Sammy did hardly anything
but sleep and dream.

Even the other sloths
began to think
Sammy was too sleepy.
"Something will have to be done
about that boy," said Mr Sloth.
He slowly scratched his head.
"He is *so* sleepy."
"Y-e-s," agreed Mrs Sloth, yawning.

"Yeah," said his sisters and brothers.

He's too sleepy...
(yawn)...to be true.

The rest of the Sloth family
closed their eyes
and sl-o-w-ly thought about it.
A week later they came up
with a plan.

Every time Sammy closed his eyes
somebody woke him up.
First Mr Sloth poked him
with a long stick.

Then Mrs Sloth shook the branch Sammy was hanging from.

Then his brothers and sisters
threw things at Sammy
or tickled him
under the arms
or called him names.

Poor Sammy didn't get
a minute's peace.
He had never been awake
for so long.
Then a funny thing happened.
Sammy didn't get more tired
from having less sleep.
He got more and more lively.

Sammy's eyes opened wide.
He stopped yawning.
He began to get bored.
He looked for something to do.
Soon Sammy's family were sorry
they had tried to keep Sammy awake.

Sammy stole Mr Sloth's paper.
He made paper aeroplanes
out of it.

Every time Mr Sloth
tried to have a nap
Sammy aimed one to land
on his dad's nose.
"Hee-hee-hee," thought Sammy.

As soon as Mrs Sloth dozed off,
Sammy began to undo her knitting.
He swung from branch to branch
with his mum's ball of wool.
He wrapped it round the branches
and round everyone else.
They looked as if
they were caught
in a giant spider's web.
"Hee-hee-hee," thought Sammy.

Sammy sneaked up on his brother.
Sid was listening
to his personal stereo.
Sammy turned the volume down.
Sid turned it back.

Sammy turned
it down again.

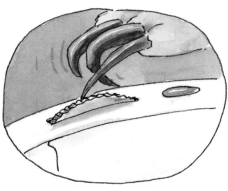

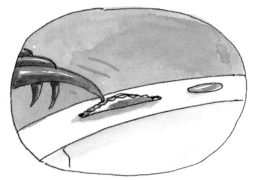

Sid turned
it back.

Sammy turned the volume *up*,
as loud as it would go.
Sid thought his ears would burst.
"Hee-hee-hee," thought Sammy.

Sammy swung up close to his sister.
Susie was reading an exciting book.
"Read me a story," said Sammy.
"Go away," said Susie.
"Go on, tell me what happens,"
said Sammy.
"Get lost," said Susie.

"Tell me when you get to
the exciting bit," said Sammy.
"Now," said Susie.

"Whoops," said Sammy.
He knocked the book
out of her toes.
It fell down...

down...

down...

down...

all the way to the ground.
"Hee-hee-hee," thought Sammy.

But worse still, Sammy waited
until his whole family
were just dropping off to sleep.
Then he shouted, really loudly,

Quick! Quick!
The tree's on fire!

When they heard *that*
even the sloths moved quickly!
Well...quicker than usual.
Sammy's family were sorry
they had ever woken Sammy up.

"Something will have to be done about that boy," said Mr Sloth, slowly rubbing his nose.

He's too lively.

"Y-e-s," agreed Mrs Sloth, yawning.

"Yeah," said his sisters and brothers.

The whole family were
looking at Sammy.
He tried to swing off.
But Mr Sloth reached out
and took hold of Sammy.

He rocked him back and to,
back and to,
back and to,
in his huge arms.

Mrs Sloth told Sammy
a gentle bedtime story.
Sammy's sisters and brothers
hummed and sang a lullaby.
The whole Sloth family
stayed very quiet
until Sammy went to sleep.

Then they all hung there: sleeping and dreaming, dreaming and sleeping... *(yawn)*...sleeping and...*(yawn)*...dreaming.

They had no idea
that Sammy was dreaming about
setting off alarm clocks,

blowing trumpets very loudly,

shaking football rattles

and bursting the biggest balloon
in the world.

He couldn't wait for tomorrow.
"Hee-hee-hee," thought Sammy.

# Crack-A-Joke

What's white, fluffy and hangs around in trees?
**A meringue-utan!**

What should you do if you find a sloth sleeping in your bed?
**Sleep somewhere else!**

How many speeds does a sloth have?
**Slow, dead-slow and stop!**

Why can't you play cards in the jungle?
**There are too many cheetahs!**

# Jokes worth hanging around for!

Why don't grapes snore?
**Because they might wake up the rest of the bunch!**

How does a sloth waltz?
**Slow, slow, slow-slow, slow!**

What goes from branch to branch wearing a bowler hat?

A bank manager!

# ANIMAL
## CRACKERS

## COLLECT ALL THE
## ANIMAL CRACKERS BOOKS!

| | | |
|---|---|---|
| A Birthday for Bluebell | 978 1 40830 293 4 | £4.99 |
| Too Many Babies | 978 1 40830 294 1 | £4.99 |
| Hot Dog Harris | 978 1 40830 295 8 | £4.99 |
| Sleepy Sammy | 978 1 40830 296 5 | £4.99 |
| Precious Potter | 978 1 40830 297 2 | £4.99 |
| Phew Sidney | 978 1 40830 298 9 | £4.99 |
| Open Wide Wilbur | 978 1 40830 299 6 | £4.99 |
| We Want William | 978 1 40830 300 9 | £4.99 |

All priced at £4.99

Orchard Colour Crunchies are available from all good bookshops, or can be
ordered direct from the publisher:
Orchard Books, PO BOX 29, Douglas IM99 1BQ
Credit card orders please telephone 01624 836000
or fax 01624 837033 or visit our internet site: www.orchardbooks.co.uk
or e-mail: bookshop@enterprise.net for details.
To order please quote title, author and ISBN
and your full name and address.
Cheques and postal orders should be made payable to 'Bookpost plc.'
Postage and packing is FREE within the UK
(overseas customers should add £2.00 per book).
Prices and availability are subject to change.